KARACTERISM

Karacterism

Copyright © 2022 by Eyleen French

Published in the United States of America

ISBN   Paperback: 978-1-959761-15-0
ISBN   eBook: 978-1-959761-16-7

All rights reserved. No part of this publication may be reproduced, stored in a retrieval system or transmitted in any way by any means, electronic, mechanical, photocopy, recording or otherwise without the prior permission of the author except as provided by USA copyright law.

The opinions expressed by the author are not necessarily those of ReadersMagnet, LLC.

ReadersMagnet, LLC
10620 Treena Street, Suite 230 | San Diego, California, 92131 USA
1.619.354.2643 | www.readersmagnet.com

Book design copyright © 2022 by ReadersMagnet, LLC. All rights reserved.
Cover design by Kent Gabutin
Interior design by Daniel Lopez

KARACTERISM

EYLEEN FRENCH

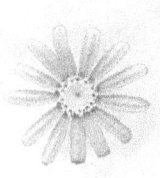

January 24, 2000

*My heart aches from
what I have seen.
People left **dying**.
People crying.
People sighing
Stunned beyond recognition.
Hearts breaking.
Love in the making.
Taken without **warning**.
Lives taken people
mourning.
What I have done
in my life, the thought
of it cuts like
a knife.*

I've finally **allowed** *the* **Lord** *to change my life. Now I'm crying for you, He can change your life too. Hear, believe, repent, confess, and be* **baptized**, *that's all you must do.*

February 3, 2000

<u>Starvation</u>

You can always buy beauty, but you can't buy salvation. So many die of spiritual starvation. We must remember to pray for our dying Nation. God puts us on probation. When we sin we must pay. Immediately following sin, we must repent and pray. To be growing, we must be in communication with Him every day. Lend a hand to anyone who is a stray. Hobos are everywhere, lend a hand show you care. Take them off the street. Give them something nutritious to eat. Say; take a load off your feet, have a seat.

February 25, 2000

I want to walk with you in the sun.
I want to run with you in the rain.
I want to be something I'm not, then people will say, "You've grown a lot.
I'm a hobo you see, that's as far as people see."

February 28, 2000

I hope to be pretty to some.
I'm just a girl, my heart has become quite numb.
The talent I have could fit in my thumb.
Some might say I'm even dumb.
I have the ability to love.
God says to be like a dove.
Plenty of time I'm still in my prime.
Please help and see some beauty in me.

March 2, 2000

"A hobo's dream"

Hobos dream, while sitting beside a stream.
The reason I know. I'm a hobo.
Looking inside, parts of me have died.
Looking back, there are things I lack.
The parts of me that have died have caused me to lose my pride.
So you see, hobos too, fight to be free.
As you go through life look upon others with kind eyes.
For as you go through life more of loves qualities you'll begin to realize.
And if you're not a hobo someday you might see there's more than meets the eye.
That you can count on till the day you die.

February 3, 2000

"God holds us forever"

No one holds on to us forever but God.
Be baptized and you'll see you'll be cleansed, sin free.
Repent is what you do and your dreams will come true.
Even for Hobos like me, it's as easy as one, two, three.
The reason I say three is the third command; believe in God.
He loves best, even when he puts us to the test.
Even a hobo can understand the meaning of command.
All the miracles of each day to count would be like counting the grains of sand in a man's hand.
Let God hold yours.

February 5, 2000

"The God Given Temple"

When you first smoke you choke.
Why do you think that is, to know you don't have to be a wiz.
It's true we all die, but it's not our call it's His.
If you start, your taxing your one and only heart.
Pollution to the lung.
Cancer no one knows when.
We know some of the cause.
Let this hobo be your friend and wound gauze.
With love you can overcome.
That goes for all not just some.

February 3, 2000

"Tick Tock"

If man goes by his own inspiration is it divine?
When I think of human response chills run down my spine.
When people look at me I often wonder what they see.
Hobos get stares.
Causing emotional fears.
Actions of some unawares.
Tick tock goes our spiritual clock, as we criticize and mock.
Take a step towards compassion and help the lame lamb walk.
Then you will see, then you will become more free.
Share hands with humanity.

March 13, 2000

"Start Now!"

Make the best of your life while your young.

Be sure you're on a path that leads to where you want to go.

Because believe me, you don't want to be a hobo.

Take your place in this word.

Be, live, believe.

And then for those of you that got a late start, let the good Lord change your life, let him lead your heart.

For all who hear, believe, repent, confess, and are baptized for the redemption of your sins. (Forgiveness for your wrong doings.)

God loves you no matter who you are.

Let him be your guiding star.

Let the warmth of his love circulate through your being.
Lift up your hands and sing.
Simply give and forgive your fellow man.
It's all part of Gods plan.
Shake someone's hand and say believe, you can.
Yes, believe and you can.
Welcome.

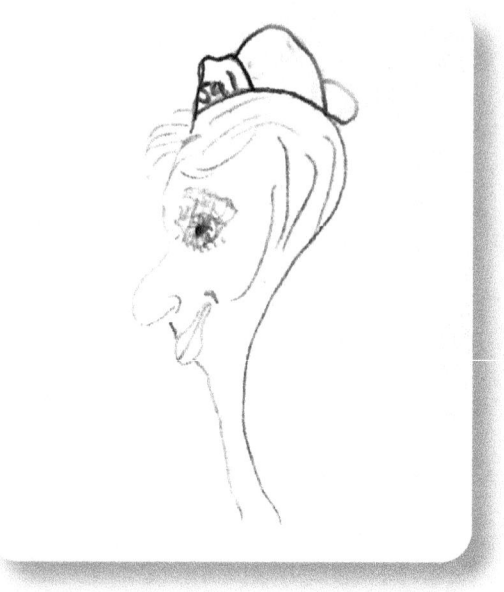

March 15, 2000

"Love is"

Love is the shadow of your heart.

Ever reminding you of sacrifice.

Time showing your hearts causing you to think twice.

Love is something that can't be tested on Laboratory mice.

The secret of love is man can feel it.

It's important to know that true love when watered can do nothing but grow.

What is your circumstance?

Do you want to dance with me?

You will truly be free.

Take it from the top.

Do you feel loved or just used or like a dirty mop?
Do you listen to hobos or, people who say this is how it goes?
Let the motion of life made by God guide you to the end.
The end to some is just the beginning.
You're on your way don't forget to pray!
Trust God with your life, after all he created it.

March 21, 2000

"Live and Love"

Think of all the people you've not yet met.

If you take your life, you'll always be in debt.

Do you want others to remember you by and by, or do you want them to say, "Why, oh why did he Choose to die?"

Remember this, there is only one you.

So explore, wisdom is nothing to ignore!

God says we could live four score and seven years so forge on, forget your fears.

Choose to live, and forgive.

The hardest one, you might find, is to forgive yourself.

Love and Care, fight despair. Put your life in God's Care.

God's right next to you. He's everywhere.

Love and live long.

Let your heart sing a never ending song.

March 28, 2000

"In My Life"

While I'm here, I want people to know I'm sincere.
I want to be an example for others to follow.
I want others to know, they don't have to be alone and hollow.
God is the cure, with him you can endure, and be secure.
Hobos care in spite of despair.
I want to spread love all around.
I want to make a love's sound.

I want to plant a love's seed.
Hoping others will water.
I want to rescue a son and a daughter.
I want to make a difference.
I want to make a change; I want to re-arrange.
I want to help husband and wife.
I want to make a difference for life.
I want to learn how to love like our Heavenly Father above.
I want to help someone inside I want them to know they're God's bride
I want them to know that their Father who rose for them, was crucified.

March 16, 2000

"First Be What You Ought To Be"

To be just what you ought to be, Live free.
Concurring what you will, dreams to fulfill.
Clear your mind, peace you will find.
The only true way, is give thanks and pray.
If anyone knows, it's us hobos.
Remember, the birth celebrated in December.
In memory of, the good Lord above.

There is hope for the least of us.

Remember, the rules, for happiness you've got the tools.

Your hands have the ability; your soul has the agility.

The last shall be first; you say.

"Oh not me I'm the worst."

But you've got the hunger, you've got the thirst.

Put those hands to use, stop the abuse.

Hug a friend, instead, that's when the abuse can see its end.

Live and love.

Pray to the good Lord Heavenly Father above.

April 10, 2000

"Make What You Do Count"

"Spend your time wisely", that's what they say.
"Make what you do count," there's no better way.
Lean on the Lord.
Obey the gospel, eternal life, will be your reward.
Look at life's beauty and splendor.
Be genuine not a pretender.
Take time to be intimate with the one you love.
For that love, thank the good Lord above.

www.ingramcontent.com/pod-product-compliance
Lightning Source LLC
LaVergne TN
LVHW021051100526
838202LV00082B/5457